DARIA PEOPLES

Hello, Mister Blue

Greenwillow Books
An Imprint of HarperCollinsPublishers

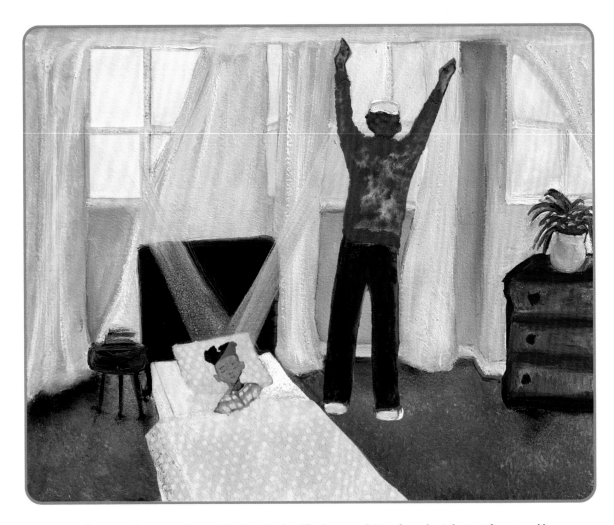

Library of Congress Cataloging-in-Publication Data is available.

ISBN 9780063206755 (hardback)

23 24 25 26 27 RTLO 10 9 8 7 6 5 4 3 2 1   First Edition   Greenwillow Books

To my parents,
Thank you for showing me how to see and know and love my neighbor.

When I stay with my papa, we walk to breakfast.

If you can keep a secret, I'll tell you . . .

Papa lets me sip his creamy, sweet coffee.

After breakfast,

we make music.

Today I meet Papa's friend.

Mister Blue lives outside.

Papa says they go back.

All the way back.

They went through some weary days
and some looking-up days
and some just-gotta-keep-pushing days.

Papa says, all day long, for all of his years,
his friend has been playing, giving the gift of his music,
a *WOMP*, a *STOMP*,
a too-good-not-to-move groove,
a funky beat with an important word to speak!

His music makes all the people in the street . . .

RISE! MARCH!

AND . . .

BOOGIE!

Papa says his friend is a working man, a moving man,
a get-up-and-go kind of brother.
But I have questions. Lots of questions.

"Is he safe?"

"Is he scared?"

"Is he lonely?"

"Is he cold?"

"Is he wet?"

"Is he hungry?"

"Hello, Mister Blue."

"Please come inside with us."

Mister Blue is my favorite musician.

And now he's my friend, too.

Author's Note

One of my father's favorite things is telling me stories about all the different people he has met in his lifetime—from his childhood, his experience in Vietnam, and his trips to visit family in Compton, California, where he met a man named Mister Blue.

Daddy never knew too many details about Mister Blue's background, but he remembered his face, and his name, and how Mister Blue loved to play the harmonica and many other musical instruments for his community.

The Mister Blue in this book is a fictional character with a fictional history, but the idea I wanted to convey was the same as in Daddy's story: Mister Blue, like many people in our country's unhoused population, brings light to his community. He contributes the best of who he is.

I read once that there are lookers and there are non-lookers—those who choose to see and those who choose not to see. I believe children choose to look, to see, to contemplate, and to act by asking hard questions we adults don't always know how to answer.

It's important that we don't prevent children or ourselves from asking hard questions.

The little girl in this story teaches us that our hard questions have the power to open and expand our minds and hearts, so that we can explore all the possible solutions that may exist for the many different challenges in our society. Every community has a Mister Blue, and every one of us has the opportunity to meet them.